This dragon book belongs to:

....

Train Your Angry Dragon
My Dragon Books - Volume 2
Written by Steve Herman

ISBN: 978-1948040075 (paperback)
ISBN: 978-1948040181 (hardcover)

www.MyDragonBooks.com

First Edition: December 2017

10 9 8 7 6 5 4 3 2 1

Train Your Angry Dragon

My Dragon Books - Volume 2

Steve Herman

Hello, my name is Andrew,
but you can call me Drew;
I have a nifty pet by the
name of Diggory Doo.

Diggory is no common pet
like a goldfish, dog, or cat
Nope, Diggory is a dragon –
Now, what do you think of that?!

Although dragon ownership is
truly pretty swell,
I have learned that it's important
to train your dragon well.

Then you must potty train your dragon and teach him how to play.

For instance, when I throw a ball, ole Diggory can catch it...

Throw a stick a country mile,
and I betcha he will fetch it!

But a dragon is much different from any other pet,
For dragons have a temper and they pose a flaming threat.
Have you ever seen a dragon when he doesn't get his way?
He throws a temper tantrum that is sure to ruin your day!

When you see an angry dragon,
you don't want to be around.
For anything that's in his way,
he'll burn it to the ground!

First he huffs and puffs;
then he fills his lungs with air...

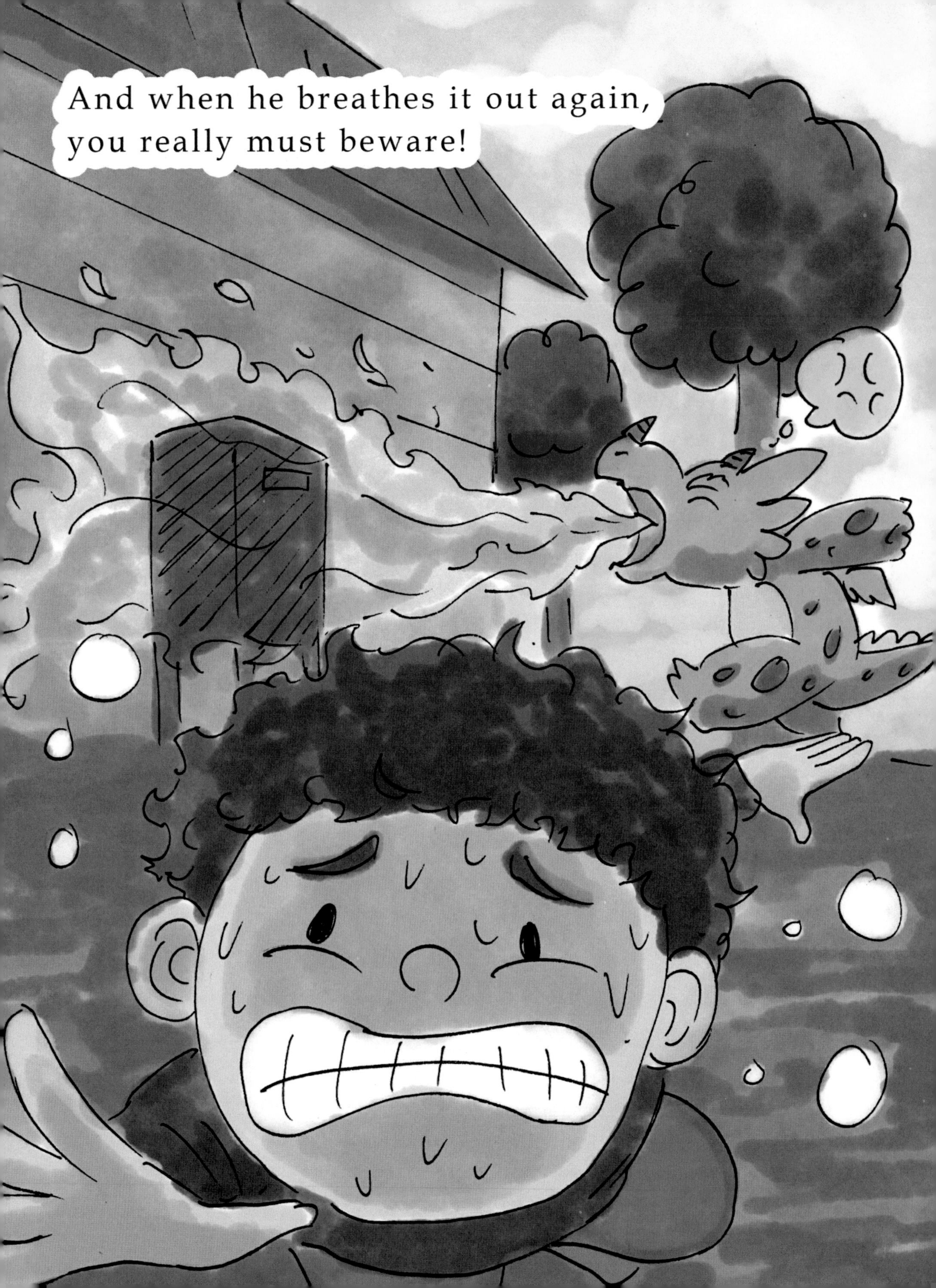
And when he breathes it out again, you really must beware!

Diggory loves the swings
and slides and seesaws at the park;
He could play there all day long
from morning until dark.

He began to look around for something he could burn!

So I said, "When you must wait,
here's something you can do --
Think of all the times that
someone had to wait on you."

One day we met some other boys,
but they weren't very nice;
Diggory nearly lost his cool,
so I gave him some advice...

"When you meet a bully,
there's no reason you should stay;
Don't burn them to a crisp
– just turn and walk away!"

Like other dragons, Diggory
hates when someone tells him, "No,"
Like "No cookies before dinner,"
or "No, you may not go."

"When you don't get your way,
slowly count to Ten,
It gives you time to calm yourself
– You'll feel better then!"

So Diggory stomped his feet,
he pouted, and he cried...

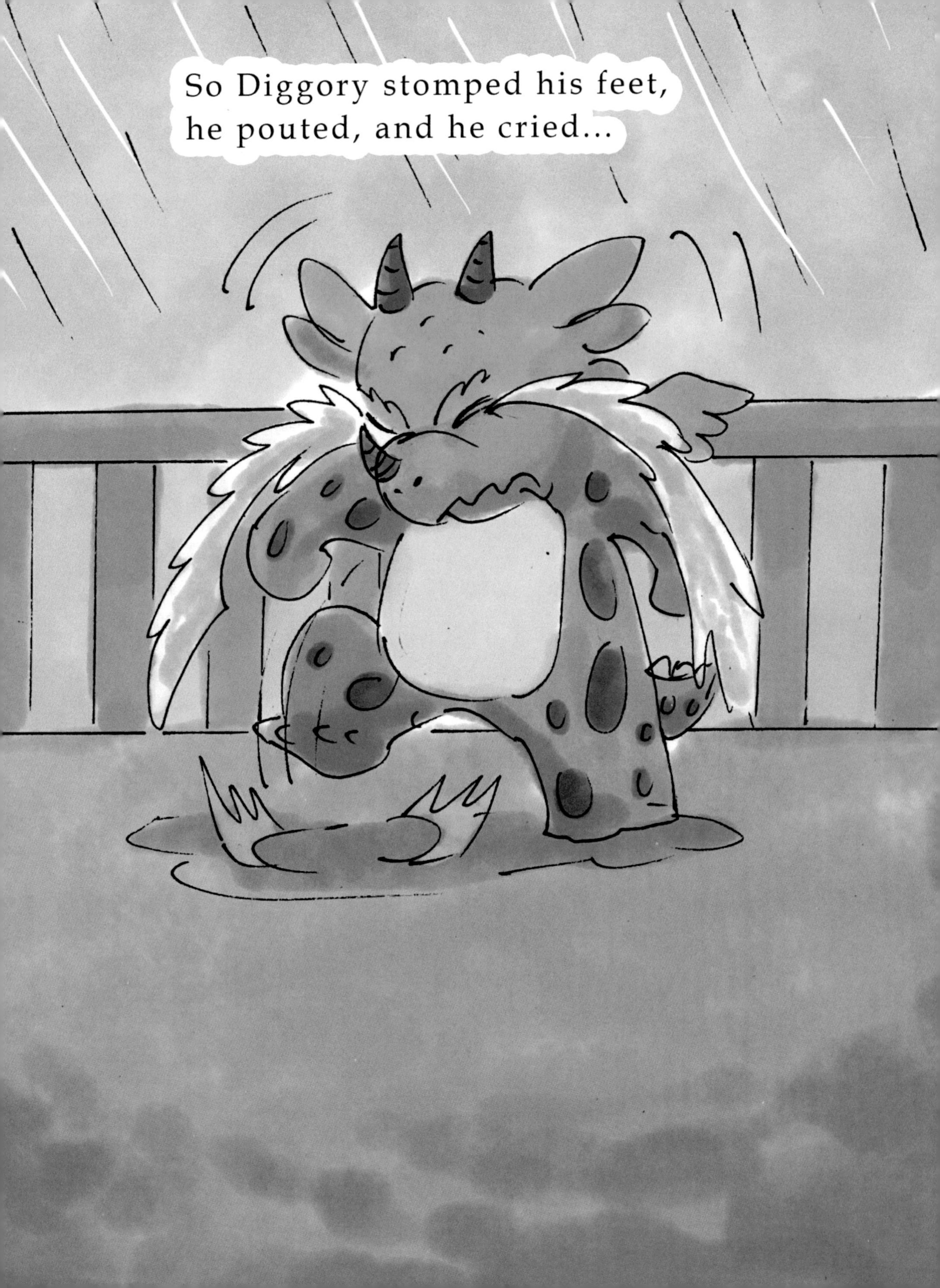

So I told him that when angry thoughts begin to fill his head, He can make them go away by thinking happy thoughts instead.

But he forgets his manners when he has to share his toys.

"Instead of getting mad,
here's what you should do...
Just treat the other children
how you want them to treat you."

A temper is the type of thing
a dragon should not lose;
That's why I taught my dragon
some tricks that he could use.

They've come in very handy
for my good friend, Diggory Doo –
Perhaps when you feel angry,
you can try them, too!

Read more about Drew and Diggory Doo!

Made in the USA
Middletown, DE
17 October 2020